the Bicklebys' BIRDBATH

For my mom and dad, who believed in me first—A. P.
To Daniele with love—R. A.

ATHENEUM BOOKS FOR YOUNG READERS • An imprint of Simon & Schuster Children's Publishing Division
1230 Avenue of the Americas, New York, New York 10020 • Text copyright © 2010 by Andrea Perry • Illustrations
copyright © 2010 by Roberta Angaramo • All rights reserved, including the right of reproduction in whole or in
part in any form. • ATHENEUM BOOKS FOR YOUNG READERS is a registered trademark of Simon & Schuster,
Inc. • For information about special discounts for bulk purchases, please contact Simon & Schuster Special Sales
at 1-866-506-1949 or business@simonandschuster.com. • The Simon & Schuster Speakers Bureau can bring
authors to your live event. For more information or to book an event, contact the Simon & Schuster
Speakers Bureau at 1-866-248-3049 or visit our website at www.simonspeakers.com. • The text for this book
is set in Providence. • The illustrations for this book were rendered in acrylic on paper. • Book design by Lauren Rille
Manufactured in China • First Edition 10 9 8 7 6 5 4 3 2 1 • Library of Congress Cataloging-in-Publication Data
Perry, Andrea. • The Bickleys' birdbath / Andrea Perry ; illustrated by Roberta Angaramo. — 1st ed. • p. cm.
Summary: A cumulative rhyme in the style of "This is the House That Jack Built," describing the antics that occur
when a girl with a long leaky hose squirts a flock of curious crows. • ISBN 978-1-4169-0624-7 • [1. Stories in
rhyme. 2. Birdbaths—Fiction. 3. Gardening—Fiction.] I. Angaramo, Roberta, ill. II. Title. • PZ8.3.P4249Bi 2010
[E]—dc22 2009009987

the Bicklebys'
BIRDBATH

by
Andrea Perry

illustrated by
Roberta Angaramo

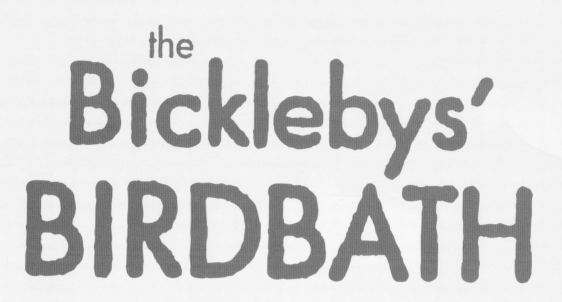

ATHENEUM BOOKS FOR YOUNG READERS
New York   London   Toronto   Sydney

This is the Bicklebys' birdbath.

This is the mailman
who fell in
the Bicklebys' birdbath.

This is the goose

that chased
the mailman

who fell in the Bicklebys' birdbath.

This is the moose

that scared the goose
that chased the mailman
who fell in the Bicklebys' birdbath.

This is the bee

that stung the moose

that scared the goose
that chased the mailman
who fell in the Bicklebys' birdbath.

This is the boy with the runny red nose
who sneezed on the bee

that stung the moose
that scared the goose
that chased the mailman
who fell in the Bicklebys' birdbath.

This is the yard
where the long green grass grows
that was mowed by the boy
with the runny red nose
who sneezed on the bee
that stung the moose
that scared the goose
that chased the mailman
who fell in the Bicklebys' birdbath.

This is the scarecrow in nifty new clothes
that fell in the yard
where the long green grass grows
that was mowed by the boy
with the runny red nose

who sneezed on the bee
that stung the moose
that scared the goose
that chased the mailman
who fell in
the Bicklebys' birdbath.

This is the nest full of buttons and bows
that came from the scarecrow
in nifty new clothes
that fell in the yard
where the long green grass grows
that was mowed by the boy
with the runny red nose

who sneezed on the bee
that stung the moose
that scared the goose
that chased the mailman
who fell in

the Bicklebys' birdbath.

This is the flock
full of curious crows
that spruced up their nest
with the buttons and bows
that came from the scarecrow
in nifty new clothes
that fell in the yard where the
long green grass grows
that was mowed by the boy
with the runny red nose

who sneezed on the bee
that stung the moose
that scared the goose
that chased the mailman
who fell in
the Bicklebys' birdbath.

This is the girl
with the long leaky hose

that squirted the flock full of curious crows

that spruced up their nest

with the buttons and bows

that came from the scarecrow

in nifty new clothes

that fell in the yard

where the long green grass grows

that was mowed by the boy
with the runny red nose
who sneezed on the bee
that stung the moose
that scared the goose
that chased the mailman
who fell in
the Bicklebys' birdbath.

This is the boy,
his pet goose by his side.

He's helping the mailman
get toweled and dried.

The mailman wraps tape
on the hose with the crack.

Scarecrow is raised from
the ground and put back.

Inside their package the Bicklebys find

a brand-new blue birdbath
that's one of a kind.

They fill it with water,
the moose cools his snout,

and off goes the mailman
to finish his route.